AN UNEXPECTED CHRISTMAS

By

Dale Warren

Unexpected Christmas

Other Books by Dale Warren

I Won a Life in the Lottery
The Vietnam War Draft Lottery - 2012

The Lizardman and Peculiar People - 2017

Hand Painted Ornaments - 2017

Copyright © 2018 Thomas Dale Warren

No part of this book may be reproduced or transmitted in any form or by any means, graphic, electronic, or mechanical, including photocopying, recording, taping, or by any information storage retrieval system, without the permission, in writing, from the publisher.

All rights reserved.
ISBN: 9781729331330

AN UNEXPECTED CHRISTMAS

GOD'S Gifts and Blessings

Dale Warren

Unexpected Christmas

Dedicated to all those who have followed God's call to ministry.

Thank you, Jane for being a great wife, loving mother, a super ministry partner and the perfect pastor's wife. Our five seminary children; Caroline, Dana, Serena, Daxton, and Jennifer that willingly sacrificed, so I could follow God's call to service.

This novel is inspired by the actual events during the adventure known as seminary.

Table of Contents

KID'S ONLY MEETING 7

THE OLD WHITE HOUSE 14

THE CHRISTMAS TREE – ADVENTURE 44

THE RESCUE 68

THE CARD – THE GIFT – THE BLESSING .. 84

AN APPLE IN YOUR STOCKING 93

MY TESTIMONY 102

Unexpected Christmas

ACKNOWLEDGMENTS

This is a work of fiction inspired by true events. Any resemblance to individuals or events is either divinely inspired, accidental, or the result of faulty memory or imagination.

I give special thanks to my family and friends, who without their prayers and assistance our adventure in seminary would have been a disaster.

All scripture quotations, unless otherwise indicated, are taken from the Holy Bible, New International Version®, NIV®. Copyright © 1973, 1978, 1984, 2011 by Biblica, Inc.TM Used by permission of Zondervan. All rights reserved worldwide. www.zondervan.com The "NIV" and "New International Version" are trademarks registered in the United States Patent and Trademark Office by Biblica, Inc.TM

Art Work: Reagan Miller & Chase Warren

Dale Warren

KID'S ONLY MEETING

And my God will meet all your needs according to the riches of his glory in Christ Jesus. Philippians 4:19

Three teenage girls, their faces glowing from the light shining off a round beige kerosene heater in the center of a wide dark hall. All three girls are dressed in heavy flannel pajamas with wool footies rubbing their hands and alternating between warming their hands next to the heater and turning around and warming their backside. Dana the oldest Walker child, had recently turned eighteen and graduated from Goose Creek High School in May. Then two months later she moved with her family to Wake Forest for her father's first year at Southeastern Seminary and her freshman year at Louisburg College. The

Unexpected Christmas

official organizer of the family, she believed in everything having a place and everything in its place. We should have known then she would become a professional organizer removing people's clutter. Just like she would do years later in ministry, she had called a meeting to make plans for Christmas. She believed in having a definite plan. That meant, having the plans in writing with bullet points, a timetable, assignments, and a budget.

She turns around facing the heater, rubbing her hands together, and whispering the expectations for the first Christmas in Wake Forest. "You know this Christmas is going to be different. Mom and Dad don't have any money this year. They usually spoil us at Christmas with too many presents."

Caroline, Dana's trombone partner in the Goose Creek marching band, best friend, and next-door neighbor was now a freshman at NC State. When the Walkers moved to Wake Forest for seminary, she had again become a regular at the Walker home. Growing up next door she and Dana would rotate between their homes spending weekends or eating dinners. I often suspected they would check what was being served for dinner at each home before deciding where to eat. Then one evening unexpectedly she had walked into the front door of our small apartment at seminary carrying a suitcase.

Jane had asked, "Caroline are you spending the weekend?"

"No" responded Caroline. "I am moving in! Dana said it would be okay. She would share her room with me. I have all I can take of that dormitory. All they want to do is stay up all night and party. You know I have to have more sleep than the average person."

With that announcement she became a permanent member of the Walker family and part of the adventure known as seminary. One change since enrolling at NC State, Caroline had become a "Granola" an organic, sew your own clothes, vegetarian. This was before it was even a preppie fad.

"Dana do you think I don't know we are all broke! After I pay my tuition and buy books, my bank account is ZERO. Maybe we could make homemade presents this year?" Caroline stated matter of fact.

Unexpected Christmas

Dax the only boy in the Walker family living in close quarters with four girls interjected as he pushed between two of the girls for a warm spot, "I am not giving up hope. I still want a new video game console for Christmas. Are one of you girls going to make me one, when did one of you become a computer nerd that can build me a new console?"

Then Serena, our niece had joined the Walker crew a few years before after a family tragedy. Serena the lone girl in the group with dark brown hair and huge brown eyes to match. The other girls were all blondes and sometimes not just blondes in hair color. Serena was normally the serious one and not known for always being the most serene. She would walk in the door from school often shaking her head and proclaiming. "I'm not taking that crap anymore!" Serena had a keen since of fairness and anytime she felt herself or even more so a friend being bullied she was the first one to confront the culprit.

"Dax don't be ridiculous! Aunt Jane and Uncle Dale are doing the best they can." Serena stated as she pushed him to the side and kept warming by the heater.

Dax interjected. "You girls quit hogging the heater. Do you know how cold it is in that closet I have for a room?" His room was not really a closet, but it wasn't a bedroom either a smaller room something between a walk-in closet and a small bedroom. "Well, it is so cold I can see my breath when I lay in my bed and if I look under my bed the cracks in the floor are so big, I can see the ground. We could all get jobs and help out."

Serena rolling her eyes and trying to dismiss Dax as she often did stated, "What kind of jobs? We are all helping Aunt Jane cook cakes, pies, and cookies for selling. I don't see you baking or boxing cookies."

"I have a job! I work for Mrs. Ruami across the street. I'm her handyman or "guter junge". Not sure exactly what it means but she says it means good boy! I clean her yard and fix things. Mrs. Ruami is deadly with a hoe. Yesterday, we were setting squirrel traps because those darn squirrels were eating her cats' food. She calls them scoundrels, thieves, and tree rats for stealing the food. I saw a snake right next to one of the traps and she took one swing with that hoe and chopped the snakes head right off. She looked right up at me as she picked it up and threw the dead snake into her trash bag and said, 'Even Jesus didn't like vipers!'"

"You didn't tell Aunt Jane any of this did you. You know she wouldn't put up with you playing with snakes." Serena spoke with authority.

"Mom knows I work for Mrs. Ruami."

Mrs. Ruami was a widow that lived across the street and acted as a substitute grandmother to our children. Her husband had taught for years at the seminary before passing away a few years before we arrived.

"Works for Mrs. Ruami yes, but playing with snakes, no way."

"We don't play with snakes or varmints. Mrs. Ruami says, we are just eliminating any varmints that threaten the neighborhood pets or children."

We would discover years later this was the birth of the original "Wildlife Guys" nuisance animal business.

"Now look what you did! I told you to hold it down." Dana whispered as the youngest Walker girl, Jennifer came out of her room rubbing her eyes.

"What are you guys doing up in the middle of the night? How am I supposed to sleep when you are making all this noise?" Jennifer said squeezing between Dana and Caroline for her space near the heater.

Yes, "The Old White House" was very cold during the North Carolina winters but we had chosen to live in the house. The house even with all its problems, was a gift and an answer to prayer.

THE OLD WHITE HOUSE

And my God will meet all your needs according to the riches of his glory in Christ Jesus. Philippians 4:19

Our first residence when we moved to Wake Forest was one of the small student apartments on campus. The apartments were fine for most of the young families that were attending seminary, but our family had grown to seven with the additions of Caroline and Serena. Even though the apartment was tight the real challenge was bedtime for the girls, since four girls were sharing one small bedroom the sleeping arrangements were a little tricky. Dana and Caroline shared a double bed that was against one wall. Serena had a single bed against the opposite wall. Then Jennifer had a cot she kept under Serena's bed, she could slide it out to sleep on.

Dale Warren

When she slid it out it completely filled the space between the beds meaning when they went to bed the room was wall to wall girls. The girls liked to tell everyone if one of them got up during the night to go to the restroom, they all four had to get up.

The student activity center was at one time a field house for the college but today the old brick building was now the hub of activity on campus. It still housed a basketball court, but now also workout rooms, study areas, recreation rooms with large TVs and pool tables. Between school, work, and family I didn't have much time to take advantage of any of those areas. My trips through the student center consisted of a quick trip through the building to the student mailboxes in the rear of the building. I made a quick glance through the small window in my post office box. The box was empty except for a small slip of yellow paper. I opened the box and pulled out a half sheet of yellow paper with "Intercampus Memo" in bold print across the top. It was addressed to: Dale Walker, from: Dean of Students, Dr. Michael Snyder with a short message – "Please come by the Dean of Students Office or call the office for an appointment." I wondered what can this be about? I thought am I getting kicked out of school? I know I bombed that Old Testament quiz, but I thought everyone bombed that one. I thought for a moment should I go directly over to the administration building or wait until after lunch or after my classes this afternoon. No, I would not be able to eat anything or concentrate on class until I knew what this was about.

It only took a quick walk to cross campus to the administration building. I had only been in the building one other time and that was during my campus orientation tour. The building was a little intimidating. It was a large gothic looking building with wide marble stairs that led to a long porch that was the length of the building. In the center of the porch were two large double doors that opened into a huge rotunda that filled the center of the building rising three floors to a huge stained-glass ceiling. A wide circular staircase wound up to each of the three floors. The administrative offices were on the first floor, the professors' offices on the second floor, and the third floor was the executive offices including the seminary president's office. As I climbed the steps, I kept feeling more and more nervous. My dad used to say, "You're acting like a long-tailed cat in a room full of rocking chairs." When I started to circle the rotunda on the second floor landing the fourth office had the door open and on the right side of the door a black sign on the wall with silver lettering "Dean of Students – Dr. Michael Snyder". Inside the office was a small receptionist area with a young blonde woman sitting at a desk folding yellow flyers.

She looked up at me and asked, "Are you here to see Dr. Snyder? Do you have an appointment?"

"No, I had this note in my mailbox." I responded handing her the note.

With a big smile she looked up and said, "Oh, you are Dale Walker, I was expecting you!"

I thought should I go ahead and confess to whatever I had been summoned to ---- or I could just slowly back out of the office go immediately home and tell Jane to start packing. I walked around campus most days in fear of somebody coming up to me and asking me to name the books of the Bible or to name King David's sons or spell one of those Old Testament kings that I could not even begin to pronounce. I was totally intimidated by most of the young students on campus that had attended a Bible College and had already had courses in New Testament, Old Testament, and Theology. The only Bible schooling I had was several years of teaching Children's Sunday School and a few weeks of Vacation Bible School. I just kept reminding myself God had called me to this adventure and HE doesn't make mistakes.

I took a deep breath and stated, "I'm Dale Walker, I can come back later."

"No, Dr. Snyder is here. He has been waiting on you. I will let him know you are here. He'll be excited you came so quickly." She reached down, pressed the intercom button on her phone, and when it was answered she said, "Dale Walker is here to see you." After a pause, I overheard her say, "I will tell him you will be right with him."

The secretary looked up and stated, "Dr. Snyder will be right with you. Jane knows me we are in the student wives club together. My name is Debbie, my husband is in a couple of your classes, Matthew Anderson."

She must have sensed my concern. "Are you nervous about this meeting? Don't worry Dr. Snyder has been trying for days to work out the details of something for you and Jane."

"Me and Jane?" I questioned under my breath.

She responded, "He is ready now. Go on back. Don't be nervous Dr. Snyder is a really good guy."

I walked in, Dr. Snyder was sitting behind a large oak desk with a window directly behind him. One wall was covered from ceiling to floor with bookcases filled with books. The other wall was covered with framed diplomas and certificates.

"Have a seat I have been trying to do something about your housing situation." Dr. Snyder said as he motioned for me to take a seat at one of the three chairs facing his desk. "Ever since I heard about how you were trying to live in one of those small apartments with seven people, I just knew that could not continue."

"We are doing okay. It is a little tight, but we knew it would be difficult when we moved to seminary." I responded not knowing exactly where this conversation was leading. I thought, had our neighbors complained? I knew the apartments were not designed to house a large family. Would, he be asking us to move out?

"I just knew you guys needed more room and have been trying to find something. After praying about this and talking it over with President Parker." (At the seminary President Parker, the seminary president, was just a notch below God.) "I think we have come up with something. It is an old house just off campus. I am not sure how it will work until we meet with the Facilities Engineer and see if you and Jane want to try it." Dr. Snyder continued explaining as he tapped a black sharpie marker on a legal pad on his desk.

"Sure, I can ask Jane what she thinks but I guess she will want to look at it. When can we take a look at the house?"

"First, let me give you a little information before you get too excited about this or tell Jane about it. It is an old house a block from seminary. The seminary purchased the property several years ago when it became available planning to eventually tear it down and use the property for a parking lot. Since, it was purchased it has become a catch all for storing junk. We are not even sure if the house is livable. Do you still want to take a look?" Dr. Snyder tried explaining.

"I can call Jane, but I feel she will want to look at it before we decide."

"Well, call her and let's get the ball rolling. The sooner we get started the sooner we know if this will work or do, we need to continue to pray and look for something else."

After a quick call to Jane, a meeting was arranged with Mr. Morgan, the Facilities Engineer. Mr. Morgan was also my boss. I worked on campus cleaning one of the classroom buildings. It was the first job I was able to obtain after moving on campus. I usually cleaned the building late at night after all the classes would end for the day. The building consisted of twelve classrooms, four restrooms, and a lounge it all had to be cleaned and prepared before classes began the next morning. I never knew when I would get a surprise inspection from Mr. Morgan. Some of the other students that also had contracts to clean buildings would share horror stories about how Mr. Morgan would show up unexpectedly and begin one of his "white glove" inspections. Most students lived in fear of the wrath of Mr. Morgan. He was the campus enforcer, if you broke one of the housing rules or he found you in one of his building without permission you were in big trouble. Now I was going to have to take Jane and meet him at his office.

Unexpected Christmas

I had been told by Dr. Snyder to meet him at Mr. Morgan's office and we would all drive over to inspect the house together. After letting Mr. Morgan know we were there, he had grunted for us to wait outside his office for Dr. Snyder. We only waited a few minutes until Dr. Snyder drove up in one of the school's black sedans. Jane and I crawled into the back seat while Mr. Morgan sat in the passenger front seat.

Before we could even back completely out of the parking place, Mr. Morgan stated, "Dr. Snyder, I don't know if this is such a good idea. I told you this place is probably uninhabitable. It has stood vacant for at least six years and during that time all we have used it for is to store stuff that nobody wanted but was afraid to throw away."

Dr. Snyder responded, "I didn't think it would hurt to at least check it out."

"I just don't want them to get their hopes up. Plus, there is nothing in our budget to spend on this project, so if anything needs replaced or fixed, I don't know where you plan to get the money."

Luckily the drive only took five tense minutes. The house was just one block from the seminary. We pulled into the gravel driveway on the side of the house with weeds growing up through the gravel. There were truck tire ruts leading up to the front porch, where trucks had been pulling up to unload stuff into the house over the years. We got out of the car and stood in the front yard looking up at the "Old White House" that would become our home for the next three years. A white wooden clapboard house with a rusty tin roof. The steps had been repaired with a few cement blocks and a couple of missing window panes were replaced with cardboard. Dr. Snyder suggested we pray before approaching the cinder block steps that led up to a large slanted porch.

After a short prayer, Mr. Morgan pulled out a large ring of keys and grunted, "Do you still want to look inside?" As he picked out a single key, he added, "Be careful I don't want anybody to fall through the floor."

Standing on the porch Jane leaned in, put her hand on her forehead and peaked in one of the windows on the large front porch. She stood up, smiled from ear to ear, and stated. "I think the house just needs a little work and some TLC." Jane could always look at a person, object, or situation and see the potential not the limitations.

Unexpected Christmas

Unlocking the door Mr. Morgan stepped in first to a large living room with a huge fireplace that had been boarded up. The living room was crowded with old furniture, file cabinets, and office equipment. That left only a small path to walk through the living room to the back of the house.

Mr. Morgan waved his hand and said, "If you guys move in, we will move all this stuff out of here as you can see nobody has lived in here for years. If we didn't have any place to put all this junk, we just stuck it here. I guess I will have to find a place for all this or dispose of it."

Jane looking at a group of old small dormitory desk stated, "If you are going to get rid of any of these desks, I could use one for each of my girls. With only one bathroom, they can't put on make-up in the bathroom and they can use these as vanities in their rooms."

"Sure, anything you can use please keep that will be less for me to have to move. Just tag it and if you want it, we can coordinate with you, so you can be here when we start moving it out. But first you need to check out the rest of the house. I am still not sure this will work."

Jane asked, "Who lived here? I am sure great memories were made on some cold nights in front of those fireplaces." The house had four large fireplaces that had all been boarded up, a few of them had become homes to different animals. We discovered this after we moved in and began hearing strange sounds in the walls.

"Dr. Bruner lived in this house with his family. He was one of the favorites around here. They say he would sit on that porch spend hours discussing theology and Christian ethics while telling students stories about his family. They had escaped from Nazi Germany when he was a young child and how his father had been a great theologian before World War II and a personal friend of Dietrich Bonhoeffer."

I was beginning to sense a transformation in Mr. Morgan. He was known for being hard as nails. If something ever got broken in one of the buildings on campus, you had better hope it wasn't your fault or you would get the wrath of Mr. Morgan. He had been known to bring more than one student to tears for breaking one of his precious pieces of furniture. But just as I have witnessed over the years that little redheaded, blue-eyed,

Unexpected Christmas

lady could melt the hardest hearts. She always saw people as special and over our years of ministry, I saw her get people to accomplish things they never dreamed possible. Yes, a transformation was beginning with Mr. Morgan. First, I noticed his voice becoming softer and even a bit of optimism in his tone.

"Mrs. Walker, I can get some of my fellows over here with some paint I had left over from the dorms we painted this summer and a fresh coat of paint on these walls would brighten this place right up. I also noticed there isn't a water heater in the kitchen. I think somebody told me the old one was taken out because it was leaking but I am pretty sure I can round up a used one from somewhere on campus that will work." Mr. Morgan explained as he pulled an old desk chair down from a stack of chairs. He pulled the chair down, wiped off the seat, and motioned for Jane to sit.

"I am fine." Jane responded as she looked in each bedroom and saw that each of the large rooms had its own fireplace. The walls needed some holes patched and a coat of paint.

Mr. Morgan insisting Jane sit in the chair he had positioned for her. He pulled another chair from the stack and without wiping this one off. He motioned to Dr. Snyder to sit down. "Dr. Snyder and Mrs. Walker let's look at our calendars and see when we can get you guys moved in to your new home. I never thought this would work but for you little lady, I am sure we can get this done and done quickly."

Dr. Snyder had a look on his face that reflected the same thing I was thinking. Is this the same Mr. Morgan we know from campus? He was smiling and actually sounding enthusiastic as he made plans with Jane to convert the old white house to a home. The house was a special gift. A special unexpected gift that would give our family the room they needed.

Once the house was pronounced as livable or somewhat livable. We began the process of moving across campus. One thing about the seminary community was that constantly new people were moving in and others moving out to their next ministry assignment. So anytime a U-Haul showed up or a pick-up truck loaded down with usually mix match furniture the neighbors would show up ready to help load or unload.

Unexpected Christmas

Sometimes these turned into all day parties. This was going to be an extra special day because the crew would be able to help load and move across campus and unload the same stuff. Of course, Jane had fixed a huge pot of chili and the best cornbread ever baked that she still baked in a cast iron skillet ready for all those that helped. Of course, no chili or cornbread until every piece of furniture and box were unloaded and the beds were reassembled. Then everyone could sit around eat chili and drink "sweet" tea while everyone shared their moving "war" stories.

A few weeks after moving into the "Old White House", it was beginning to shape up into a home. The four bedrooms worked well. The three large bedrooms allowed one for Jane and me: one for Dana and Caroline: one for Jennifer and Serena, and the small one for Dax. The fall had been the perfect time to move into the house since it didn't have air conditioning or heat. The days were a little warm, but fans placed strategically kept it livable and the nights were cool but comfortable. Jane and I didn't know what to do about the coming winter, but we trusted God would supply our needs.

And my God will meet all your needs according to the riches of his glory in Christ Jesus.
Philippians 4:19

Jane standing in the middle of the small kitchen said, "Somebody answer the door! I have my hands full finishing up supper."

Jennifer jumped up, opened the heavy wooden front door and turned back towards the kitchen announcing, "It's Uncle Dale and Aunt Kim!"

Jane responded, "WHAT? Well, let them in." She wiped her hands on her apron stepped into the hall where she could see from the back of the house right up the center of the house to the front door. "Dale, this is unexpected, you could have called, and I would have fixed something special for supper."

Jane had married a Dale and her closest brother was also a Dale. Dale and Kim were Jane's brother and sister-in-law that had become our closest friends. Not just because Jane and Uncle Dale were only a year apart and had grown up very close. After we had gotten out of the army our families became even closer. We were neighbors, our children grew up together, and we even took vacations together. I often share with others my brother-in-law Dale was very important to me. He not only introduced me to Jane, but also introduced me to Jesus. How could somebody have a more important influence on your life than to introduce you to the love of your life and your Lord and Savior. *

"I am glad you didn't. I brought supper. It's in the truck." Dale responded. "Dax and Jennifer go out to the truck and bring in the supper. Jane, you do have some tea made don't you."

"Yes, I have plenty of tea, but what did you bring for supper."

Kim spoke up, "He stopped and got Kentucky Fried Chicken. I told him to get something healthy, but you know your brother if it ain't fried and greasy he doesn't want it."

Kim and Jane had been on a lifelong struggle to make the two Dale's eat healthy. Fried food, gravy, barbeque pork, and sweet tea is part of our heritage and any attempt to change a southern redneck's eating habits are nearly impossible. We all sat down shared a huge meal and many laughs, as we did every time members of this family got together to share a meal.

After dinner Uncle Dale sat back in his chair and said, "This house certainly gives you much more room than that little apartment we helped you move into back during the summer. I heard from Nana about your new home, but she was worried because you didn't have any heat."

Jane responded, "We have some electric heaters we can put around."

Uncle Dale quickly added, "Those things are dangerous plus once winter hits North Carolina those heaters will not keep this old house warm.

Unexpected Christmas

Kim and I talked about this last week, so we have brought you a couple of kerosene heaters and some cans for storing kerosene. They still won't keep this house toasty when it gets freezing, but at least you want freeze to death in here."

After a quick survey of the house Kim stated, "Let's stop talking about it and get those heaters in, set them up and show Dale and Jane how to operate them. Even with the heaters, this house needs a lot of work for me to feel comfortable. There are broken windows. In the bathroom the sink is cracked, and the faucet has a constant leak. There is no insulation in this house and many other things that could be fixed easily."

Jane explained, "We are making it work. It's not perfect but it is better than the little apartment – at least we are not on top of each other."

Kim looked at Uncle Dale and yelled, "I got it! I will send Carlos up here with his toolbox and my Lowes card and in a week; he could do miracles. What do you think Dale? Can he come up here next week? Jane can make a list of projects and Carlos will knock it out in no time."

Uncle Dale realized, these weren't really request. Once Kim got an idea in her head and that tone in her voice there was no stopping her. He realized this was one of those times when he should remember the advice, he gave to every young groom he ever met on the eve of their wedding. Just remember two little words and your marriage will last forever. Those two little words "Yes Dear!"

It was settled. Kim would send Carlos to fix up the "Old White House". Now Carlos had worked on roofs for Uncle Dale for over thirty years before he decided it would be the best thing for his insurance and for Carlos for him to retire from roofing. Dale couldn't just let Carlos go, he had become a part of the family being one of the first roofers to work with him. Carlos had always been loyal, good times or bad. Dale had called him into his office several years earlier. Carlos shared many times he knew it was time and was sure Mr. Dale, as he always referred to him was going to have to let him go since he could no longer work safely on the roofs. But Dale had another job or as Dale like to call it mission for him. Dale explained to Carlos don't thank me yet, but I do have another position. Tomorrow I want you to report to my house, Kim has a few projects I just don't have time to do.

Unexpected Christmas

For the next ten years, Carlos had become Kim's right hand man. They had a strange relationship. Even though Carlos had a Hispanic background he had been born in Charleston and spoke English better than many of the seminary students. Now when it came to Kim, Carlos could not speak one word of English and any misunderstanding about Kim's expectations or directions and what Carlos did to complete the projects was certainly a result of a miscommunications between him and Kim. Watching the two of them communicating was one of the most entertaining things to watch in Goose Creek. Kim would use exaggerated hand motions and speak English and broken Spanish usually very loudly. Carlos would shake his head up and down and say in a very strong Spanish accent "OK Miss Kim, I fix it". Then he would pick up his toolbox. They would both walk away shaking their heads.

Kim put her arm around Jane's waist pulled her a little closer and said directly to her Dale, "You okay with sending Carlos up here to fix this place up for your "little" sister?"

"Sure – Sure, soon as we get home, we can check his schedule and coordinate between Jane and

Carlos when he can come and what he needs to do," Dale responded.

Two weeks later, Carlos arrived in his large black GMC truck with ladder rack carrying a steel extension ladder and a large silver tool box behind the cab of the truck. Jane met him at the door in her jeans a white blouse and blue apron.

"Carlos come on in, I was in the kitchen. We have been baking a wedding cake for a wedding this Saturday. I am right at a critical point and can't stray away from the stove." Jane explained as Carlos followed her back to the small galley kitchen.

"Can I fix you a glass of tea? I know you must be tired, thirsty, and hungry from the drive up."

"Sure, I will take that tea, but I am fine. I want to rest a few minutes then I will look around and see where we need to begin in the morning." Carlos explained as he sat down at the round dinner table in the corner of the kitchen.

The table was covered with a beige table cloth with a large round container of icing and a small bride and groom statue in the center. Just as he sat down, he asked Jane if he could use her phone to call Kim and let her know he had gotten to Wake

Forest and was ready to go to work. Jane lifted a yellow portable wall phone off the receiver and handed it to Carlos.

As Jane peeked in the oven she said, "Carlos, you better check in before Kim calls the highway patrol."

Carlos cleared his voice and switched from the perfect English to his broken English with a strong Spanish accent as he dialed Kim's phone. "Miss Kim, I here – with Miss Jane – Going to work now – I call tomorrow."

Carlos stood up and handed the phone to Jane. "Kim, Carlos just got here I fixed him a glass of tea and will show him around as soon as I take this cake out of the oven. Thanks again for sending him, I am sure he will make a big difference around here. I'll call you tomorrow and give you an update on the progress."

Jane paused as Kim stated, "Don't run up your phone bill but if you need anything give me a call. I gave Carlos the Lowes credit card and told him if he needs any supplies just get what he needs but keep the receipts."

"Thanks again, I better go before I burn this cake. Give Dale my love." Jane said as she hung-up the phone.

Jane pulled the three layers of cake out of the oven and sat them down very carefully as if lying a sleeping baby down in a crib. The cakes were her baby and Jane took great pride in the cakes she prepared for birthdays, weddings, anniversaries, and other special events. Jane's cakes quickly gained a reputation around the campus and anytime a dignitary visited the campus or there was a special celebration, President Parker's wife always reminded anyone on campus to order the cake from Jane.

After setting down the cakes Jane turned to Carlos, "I am going to let you sleep in Dax's room. You can use his bed and I can put a cot in there for Dax."

"You don't have to do that, I brought a sleeping bag and can just find a corner."

"No, you aren't sleeping on the floor. Dax has been waiting on you. He told me he helped you with some work before we moved, and he can't wait to be your assistant again. He will be excited to share his room with you."

Unexpected Christmas

Jane showed Carlos through the house pointing out a few obvious problem areas. The bathroom sink, and vanity were in bad shape, there was a cracked window in the kitchen, and a few other projects. Jane informed Carlos that Mr. Morgan had told her he had located a faucet, sink, and vanity for the bathroom. They weren't new but were in good condition.

"In the morning Dale can take you by the maintenance office and introduce you to Mr. Morgan before he goes to class," Jane explained.

"That would be great, Kim had thought I would have to purchase new stuff for the bathroom, but if that stuff will work, we can use that money for something else. If it is in bad shape or you don't like it, we will say thank you and go down to Lowes and see what we can find."

Jane responded, "Well, let's see what Mr. Morgan has first."

That night only after us demanding it Carlos slept in Dax's room on his bed with Dax using an old army cot and sleeping bag. The next morning Carlos and I grabbed a quick cup of coffee and a bagel before getting in Carlos's truck and riding over to the campus facilities offices. The office was on the opposite side of campus and about two blocks from the campus. The campus was encircled by a three-foot high stone wall that was under a constant state of repair. Nehemiah had rebuilt the wall around Jerusalem in just 52 days, but this wall repair had been going on for years. The campus buildings were all old traditional brick buildings but the facilities building resembled a World War II hangar. The large metal building was painted a dark grey color with four black garage doors lining down the side of the building. The back of the building had a large chain link fenced area with an assortment of old appliances and an old dump truck with flat tires. There was lumber, shingles, and sheets of siding stacked along the inside of the fence. At the front of the building was a standard door with a sign that read "Office" on the top. The parking place closest to the door had a small sign "Reserved – Mr. Morgan Facilities Director". We parked in the space next to the reserved space where an old red pick-up truck was parked.

As we got out of the truck, I pointed at the red truck and said, "That's Mr. Morgan's truck. He must be here already."

Unexpected Christmas

Carlos just shook his head and walked with me into the office. In the corner of the office was a large metal desk with stacks of paper covering the desk. On one corner of the desk was a dark brown leather tool belt with a well-worn leather tool pouch filled with tools. Mr. Morgan sat behind the desk in a large black leather desk chair. The leather on both chair's arms had been worn through showing what at one time had been white stuffing before many years of workers hands had turned it a dark grey.

"Mr. Morgan, this is Carlos he is going to do some work at the house." I said as Carlos reached over to shake hands with Mr. Morgan.

Mr. Morgan replied, "Yes, I spoke with your brother-in-law yesterday. We can use all the help we can get around here. He says you are a pretty good handyman. I can use that around here, sometimes I think I am the only one around here that can fix anything. These preacher boys might be book smart, but they are allergic to tools and manual labor."

Pointing to a small square table in the corner with a coffee maker and a couple of shakers of sugar and creamer, Mr. Morgan said, "Carlos help yourself to some coffee while I get some of these guys started for the day." Referring to several young men most of them students that worked part-time for maintenance that were standing around in the office drinking coffee and complaining about a few of the professors.

"Carlos, I need to go to class now, so I'll just leave you guys to figure out what you want to do." I stated as I threw my book bag over one shoulder and walked out of the door.

After a morning of classes, I returned home for lunch. I walked into the house, sat my book bag on the floor right inside of the door. "Where is Carlos? I didn't see his truck outside."

Jane responded, "I haven't seen him since he left with you this morning. I got a call around 8:30 from Mr. Morgan asking if Carlos could help him with a small project this morning. I guess he is still working on that project with Mr. Morgan."

Just as Jane finished Carlos walked in the front door. "Sorry I helped Mr. Morgan this morning. He had two apartments with leaks. I heard him trying to explain to one of the young guys in the office about the problem, but I knew that young fellow had no idea what to do. So, I told him I worked on roofs for thirty years and to let me look and see what I could do. We got both roofs fixed and Mr. Morgan promised to come over after lunch and help me install the new bathroom fixtures, since I helped him with the roof."

Carlos was originally only staying a few days and fixing a few things, but over the next month he and Mr. Morgan became a dynamic duo around campus fixing things that had been on somebodies wish list for years. Soon everywhere I would go on campus professors and students were asking me to have Carlos give them a call or come by their apartment or classroom to look at something.

Finally, Uncle Dale called and told Carlos his fun in Wake Forest would have to come to an end. Kim's to do list was getting extremely long. Jane promised to send him back in a few days, but before he could leave, Jane planned a going away party. Jane, several of her friends that Carlos had done projects for, and Mr. Morgan all decided to help throw a huge party. Mr. Morgan volunteered to bring his large trailer mounted cooker to grill burgers and everyone else brought their favorite dishes to share with this new friend that had come to complete a few projects around the old house.

He had completed the projects at the old house in addition to working all around campus fixing everything from leaky roofs, to broken windows, to dripping faucets. Yes, he was going to be missed by the seminary families. The party even had a surprise visit from Dr. Snyder and the seminary president, Dr. Parker. They arrived as the party was ending with a framed certificate of appreciation for Carlos, the man who had come to do a few odd jobs and left as one who demonstrated the spirit of servanthood. Dr. Parker told the crowd our professors attempt to teach not just theory and theology but the challenge of following Christ's example of servanthood. Carlos was a living example of that spirit of servanthood.

*(For more information about this relationship refer to "I Won a Life in the Lottery" or please read the most important aspect of this book, my personal testimony in the appendix.)

THE CHRISTMAS TREE – ADVENTURE

Keep your lives free from the love of money and be content with what you have, because God has said, "Never will I leave you; never will I forsake you." Hebrews 13:5

I knew the decision to follow God's call, sell our home, and move to seminary in Wake Forest was not a personal decision but a family decision. Those actions would affect our entire family as we left the comfort of family and home. We knew some of the perks of my corporate position our family had grown accustomed to would end. Before the Griswold's Christmas Vacation, the Walkers had for many years made a trek to the Blue Ridge Mountains over Thanksgiving weekend to discover the perfect Frazier fir tree, cut it down, and bring it back strapped to the top of our car. Our kids would all duck down below the seat trying to avoid the stares of our neighbors as we drove back home. Once something was done in the Walker family Dana made sure it became a tradition and traditions are meant to be kept. This tradition was more than just jumping in the car and driving to the nearest lot to pick out a precut tree. We would make a trip to the mountains, a several hundred-mile trip with a night or sometimes two-night stay at the perfect little bed and breakfast. Then going up to the Christmas Tree corner on the Blue Ridge Parkway, taking a wagon ride out into the field, searching for the perfect tree, cutting it down, and returning it home.

Unexpected Christmas

There was one huge difference since moving to seminary. Going to the mountains to obtain the perfect tree was expensive and we didn't have any extra money. As with most serious discussions, this one began around the dinner table just a couple of weeks before Thanksgiving, it was on a Saturday morning breakfast. Trying to coordinate dinners around class schedules, job schedules, catering jobs, study groups, etc. made family dinner times nearly impossible to schedule. Saturday morning was one of the few times the whole family could sit down and catch up over a plate of Jane's blueberry pancakes and a pile of bacon.

"Are we going back to Goose Creek for Thanksgiving?" Dax asked as he dripped some syrup on the front of his Gamecock t-shirt.

I answered as I lifted another piece of bacon. "I am not sure at this point, how we will be able to coordinate our schedules."

"How are we going to get a Christmas tree this year? Are we going to have one of those artificial trees this year?" Dana asked in a disappointed voice of reality.

Serena, who usually avoided these family discussions, she explained to me once. "Just call me Switzerland, I ain't getting between Dana and Dax or even worse Dax and Aunt Jane." Today was different. She boldly spoke up. "A fake tree, Aunt Jane ain't going for no fake tree. Are you?" Pausing and looking up at Aunt Jane waiting on her response.

Jane had got up from the table to refill my coffee mug then she responded. "Well, we might be able to go get our tree after all. Guess who called me last week and invited us up to the mountains?" Before anyone could answer, "The Whiteheads, they want us to come up over Thanksgiving weekend for free. They even offered to help with the cost of our gas to drive up, if we can come up for a visit."

The Whiteheads, Len and Lynn Whitehead were retired missionaries that owned a small bed and breakfast near Blowing Rock, North Carolina. We had been staying with them for years on our Christmas tree adventures. We loved staying in their rustic old stone home and listening to them share missionary stories late into the night.

Len loved when he introduced themselves, he always said. "We are Len and Lynn Whitehead, if you get confused just remember I am 'Len'". He would then begin to share how God had blessed them many times during their over thirty years as missionaries in the Thailand, India, and Africa before retiring to the Blue Ridge Mountains. We always looked forward to the two-night stay with them because it meant one breakfast of Lynn's Blue Berry Gingerbread pancakes and the second morning would be Len's original omelets. Plans began coming together for our annual Griswold Christmas tree adventure.

At first, we thought it would be impossible for all seven of us to be able to attend. Scheduling the time off for Dale, Dana, and Caroline from their jobs. Then we would have to make sure Jane's catering responsibilities would not be a conflict but after some prayer and several phone calls the trip was scheduled. We would leave on Friday after classes and work drive up to the Whitehead's spend the night, get-up Saturday morning and go find the perfect Christmas tree, return to the Whitehead's for Saturday night. On Sunday morning we could eat the huge breakfast and then go to church with the Whitehead's to hear Len preach before leaving to return to Wake Forest.

Thanksgiving came quickly, on Friday we loaded up the Lumina van affectionately known as the Silver Bullet. The Silver Bullet had been Jane's dream car ever since she had seen it in Future World at Disney World's EPCOT. The van had been on a display of cars that would be coming out in the future. The sloped nose and aerodynamic design made the Silver Bullet resemble a car of the future. Being a lifelong Star Trek and Star Wars fan, Jane had to be one of the first to march down and pick out one of these futuristic vehicles, when they were available in Charleston. The sleek design and silver color made the name Silver Bullet seem perfect and it didn't hurt that usually when Jane drove the Silver Bullet it got to the destination in a hurry. That Friday morning as we squeezed the family into the van it also helped that the van had seven separate bucket seats and seven cup holders.

Jane began giving orders, "Let's get this van loaded and everyone find your seat. I want to get on the road, so we can get to the mountains before dark."

With the kids all wearing jeans and an assortment of sweatshirts, Dax and Jennifer took

Unexpected Christmas

the two seats in the very back (fondly referred to as the back-back) with Dana, Caroline, and Serena sliding into the three seats in the middle. Serena quickly shouted, "I have to sit by a window. You guys know I get car sick and you don't want me barfing all over the place."

"No, Serena we don't want you barfing!" Dana interjected. "I will sit in the middle."

Jennifer quickly spoke up. "I'll sit in the middle if you sit in the back with Dax. He makes weird sounds and smells the whole trip."

Jane ordered, "Jennifer you stay right where you are. Dana take the middle and Dax, you control those bodily sounds and smells. I need this trip and a few days away from the stress. Do you guys want to start the trip with some singing?"

Dax spoke up from the back. "No, I'll just listen to my music and play with my Gameboy," as he slid his headphones over his ears and looked down at his Gameboy. The four girls all in harmony added. "Not Now!" as they each put on their headphones and tuned into their own little worlds to pass the time to the mountain respite.

Of course, Dana leaned forward between the two front seats turned her head towards Jane who was driving and whispered. "Sorry Mom I know you like for us to sing and all get along. Do you want me to make them take off their headphones and sing something?"

Jane responded, "No, Dana just sit back. I think I would just like some peace and quiet."

Peace and quiet, in a few weeks we would be celebrating the birth of the Prince of Peace and our lives over the last few months had been anything but peaceful. The weekend was a short respite from the very stressful life Jane had lived during this transition. Trying to create a new home in a very difficult situation, first too small and crowded then more room but challenging. Trying to help ends meet by earning money cooking and babysitting or saving money anyway possible. Doing everything she could to free me up, so I could spend time studying and going to classes. Yes, God was providing a very needed escape.

And the peace of God, which transcends all understanding, will guard your hearts and your minds in Christ Jesus. Philippians 4:7

Unexpected Christmas

After several hours of quiet traveling except for a few "He hit me" or "Dax is passing gas". We drove up a very steep gravel drive to a large stone home with a wooden hand-painted sign across the top it read - **Len and Lynn's Bed and Breakfast** – directly under it the verse - **"Be still and know that I am God" Psalms 46:10.** The message on their sign was exactly what we needed.

Opening the front door Lynn stepped onto the porch that had four rocking chairs to her left and a wooden rustic table with six mixed match wooden chairs encircling the table. "Jane, I was beginning to worry. These roads are a little difficult to navigate after dark."

"We are fine. I've drove that road up the side of the mountain enough times now I know where to be careful, but it sure feels good to get out that car and stretch my legs." Jane responded as she got out the car. "Okay, everyone get your own bag and bring it in the house." Jane had trained the kids to pack everything they were bringing on a trip in one backpack bag.

As we entered the front door into a sitting area with a large stone fireplace that had a full roaring fire, Jennifer and Serena headed straight for the fireplace turning around and backing up to the fire. Lynn began directing, "Kids take your bags upstairs, you know what rooms are yours, Jane, you and Dale take the large room down here. Get comfortable and come right back. I will have some hot apple cider and homemade cookies waiting for you."

Dax was already half way up the stairs. Yelling over his shoulder, "I will be right down. I love your cookies!"

Quickly everyone was back down sitting on the three couches that formed a semicircle facing the fireplace with a mug of hot apple cider and a napkin with home-made chocolate chip cookies.

Len was sitting in his rocker with a gray Blue Ridge Mountain sweatshirt, a well-worn pair of blue jeans, and his cowboy boots. "Lynn come on out of the kitchen. I want to hear all about their seminary experience."

"I am coming in there, just give me a minute to straighten up. Does anyone need a refill or some more cookies before I close the kitchen for the night?" Lynn responded as she cut out the kitchen light and walked out of the kitchen wiping her hands on her apron.

Unexpected Christmas

We spent the next two hours telling our two friends, Len and Lynn, all about our move to seminary. Jane was telling the two former missionaries, that we were beginning to understand how they felt during their years in service to the Lord. When it seemed like we would be giving up so much to go to Wake Forest, God kept providing all our needs. Gradually, Jane would send a couple of the kids at a time upstairs to prepare for bed.

And my God will meet all your needs according to the riches of his glory in Christ Jesus.
Philippians 4:19

Finally, when it was only the four adults, I took my last sip of apple cider and said, "I just want to thank you guys. I had given up any hope of coming up to the mountains for our tree this year."

Len stood up, placed his hand on my shoulder, and said, "We would have missed you guys. When you first came up here it was just another visitor, but over all these years you have become like family. Lynn could not stand the idea of going through the holidays without seeing you guys. We have seen your kids grow up. Now let's all go to bed, tomorrow morning will come early and you need to get out there and find that perfect tree."

The next morning bright and early immediately after a breakfast of gingerbread pancakes, homemade blueberry syrup, and bacon, we were on the road to the Christmas tree capital of the world. Pinenola, North Carolina was a small village not far from Blowing Rock and the Bed and Breakfast but on the winding mountain roads it took over an hour to arrive at our destination. The Christmas Tree Corner was a hub of activity. A large gravel parking lot was filled with several cars and trucks. At the back of the lot was a red barn with a large hand-painted sign across the front, **"The Christmas Tree Corner"** under the sign in smaller print, **"U-cut or we-cut trees – Free hot apple cider and hayrides"** had been added in green paint. We pulled in and parked between an old Ford blue pick-up and a new black Mercedes with a New York license plate.

Jane parked next to the Mercedes, "See they come all the way from New York here to get the perfect tree. Let's go inside use the restroom, get a cup of apple cider, and then we can take the wagon up the mountain and find a tree."

Once inside the barn there was a counter with cups of hot apple cider lined up on one end and an assortment of muffins, and breakfast pastries at the other end with a piece of paper taped to the counter saying, **"Support the Pinenola Baptist Youth Mission Trip – Suggested donation $1"**.

Jennifer and Dax holding a cup of cider with both hands said at the same time. "Can we get something to eat, pointing at a row of cinnamon rolls."

"You just ate a huge breakfast. Let's wait until after we pick out a tree. We need to get started. It has already started snowing and we must find the tree now. While they are bundling it up and putting it on the car, we can come back in here and get a snack and warm back up."

Waiting for our family parked in front of the barn was an old wooden wagon with four rows of benches across. The wagon was being pulled by a large old green John Deere tractor that had been used on the tree farm for at least a few decades of service.

The driver wearing a pair of brown coveralls and an orange University of Tennessee stocking cap pulled down over his ears. Pointing up the side of the mountain he said, "You guys jump on up on the wagon and take a seat. I will take you out to find your perfect tree. Don't sit too close to the edge of the wagon, to get to the good trees we have to go way up there and in a few places it's a little tricky."

He raced the engine and a huge puff of black smoke bellowed out of the tractor as it jerked and started up the trail behind the barn. Looking over his shoulder asking, "What kind of tree are you looking for? We have some nice white pines or spruce trees."

Jane quickly answered, "No, we only want to look at the Fraser Firs. As for me, that is the only Christmas tree. We have had a Fraser Fir every year."

"Okay, I know right where to take you to find a great Fraser. Sit back, it will take a few minutes. There are a few blankets back there if you need to wrap up."

Jennifer and Serena quickly picked up a dirty gray blanket with some unidentifiable stains and a few sprigs of straw hanging on. Sitting directly in front of them Dana turned around and said, "Put those blankets back down who knows who has wrapped up in them. They might be full of bugs or germs or who knows what?"

Jennifer looked past Dana, "Mom tell Dana she can't tell us what to do."

"Jennifer and Serena maybe it would be better to just put those back on the floor of the wagon. We will be getting off in a second." Jane explained as the wagon began slowing down.

"Here you go, I will let you out here. There is a bunch of good-looking Frasers up this hill and more over on the next hill. Don't forget your saw and I will be back to pick you up right here in a little while." He handed me a whistle and said. "If you need me back sooner just start blowing that whistle and I will hustle right back up here."

As with everything in our lives, Jane had a plan perfected to pick out the perfect tree. Each child would become a tree tag. As soon as we got off the wagon Serena freezing said, "Aunt Jane, That's a good looking one right there." Pointing to the third tree in the first row of trees.

No, it was never this easy to find a tree. One on the first row of trees, you must be kidding. No, this was just the beginning of the search. Jane would check out every tree on these five acres from every angle before a tree worthy of going in our home was found.

Jane responded to Serena's suggestion. "That one does look good, so go stand right beside it. If we don't find a prettier one, I will come back for it."

Serena went and took her post with a little bit of exaggerated shiver blowing on her hands. "Don't take all day. Uncle Dale tell her this one is just fine."

"Serena, just give us a few minutes. Jane isn't looking for fine. She is looking for the perfect tree." I answered.

About fifty-yards further up the hill, we moved over one row of trees. "This one might be a keeper. Jennifer, stand next to it, while I check out a few more."

"Mom, we are all freezing. Find one in a hurry, Dad don't forget I'm out here. I don't want to be left here by myself make Dax stay with me." Jennifer responded as she stood stomping her brown boots on the ground trying to warm her feet.

Unexpected Christmas

Dax shouted, "I can't stay. I'm carrying the saw." As he walked further up the hill.

After eliminating trees because some were too short or too tall but mostly because that one has a hole here or there. Jane's definition of a hole was an imperfection, maybe a limb was broken or a void where a limb should be to make it symmetrical. I could never figure out if one side of the tree was going in the corner or against the wall what difference did that "hole" make.

Just as Jane was eliminating another tree because of the "hole" and as a fear of frost-bitten children crossed my mind. I asked, "Jane, we can put that side in the corner nobody will ever know a hole is there."

"I'll know it is there, Thomas D!" Jane shouted back.

How many years or decades would it take for me to realize, okay or good enough was not in Jane's vocabulary. "Okay, there is some more good-looking trees on that next row."

Dax kept circling the trees anxiously swinging the saw waiting to start cutting. "Don't tell me we are going to do like we do every year."

"Quit swinging that saw before you cut off your ear and exactly how do we do it every year?" Jane asked Dax.

"We walk ten miles up and down these hills looking at every tree. Then we go back and get one of those first trees we looked at when we got off the wagon."

"Dax, you can give the saw to your Dad and go back up the trail and relieve Jennifer before she freezes if you think we are going back to cut it down anyway." Looking up Jane pointed. "That's it right there! What do you think."

Dax and I both spoke up with a sigh of relief, "Looks great!"

"Dad, do you want me to begin sawing it down?"

"Sure, just try to cut it as close to the ground as possible. We can use that extra trunk to have room to cut it again when we get it home."

Dax began the sawing and let me saw the last half. Then we dragged the tree back to the trail with a little help from the girls.

Jennifer couldn't resist, "Mom, good thing I saw Dad and Dax dragging the tree. They were three rows over. I think you guys forgot how far over you had left me. Last year you guys left me out in the field to freeze. Just in case I left you a map on the seat of the van."

JENNIFER'S CHRISTMAS TREE FARM MAP!!!

"We knew exactly where you were all the time. Believe me we would never leave you out here in the cold and we didn't leave you last year. Let's catch that wagon. You guys can warm up and get some hot apple cider while we pay and get the tree wrapped up and tied to the roof of the van." Jane explained as we watched the wagon stop and the driver jump down and help lift the tree into the wagon.

The driver pulled himself up on the seat to the John Deere stating, "I'll get you back down quickly. It's starting to snow harder, and it will get worse really quick. You will want to get this tree back down and get back on the road while you can."

He stopped the wagon at the end of the parking lot where there was a large machine used for wrapping the trees for transport. There were already several trees lined up next to the machine where two young men were feeding the trees into the machine and another two men were taking the trees once they were wrapped to the car or truck of the owners. Once at the vehicle they quickly tied the trees to the roof of the vehicle and sent the owners on their way.

Unexpected Christmas

While we unloaded off the wagon the driver said, "The cashier is inside. Grab yourself a hot cider or a coffee and we should have you ready to go in a few minutes."

Walking into the converted barn that was now an office, snack shop, and gift shop; the children headed straight over to the hot apple cider grabbing a plastic cup of cider and moving over to the large wood stove in the corner. Jane and I walked over to the cashier, an older man we had come to know from our yearly visits was manning a large old cash register on the long bare wooden table.

"I pray you found a good one this year, Miss Jane." The man behind the cash register greeted us as we walked up.

Jane reached in her coat pocket pulling out her check book. "A beauty just like every year. How much do we owe you?"

He looked back into a small kitchen behind the counter and spoke to an older woman that kept the hot apple cider flowing, stocking the cookies, and making some egg salad sandwiches. "Margaret it's the Walkers." Looking back at Jane, "Margaret told me to let her know when you came in."

Margaret and her family had grown the trees on that mountain for generations. She walked out of the kitchen in a denim dress with an old gray sweater wiping her hands on a soiled dish towel. "You weren't going to come in here and leave without catching me up on everything? I saw the kids, they are growing like weeds. What are you feeding Dax, I think he has grown a foot since last year?"

Jane responded, "I just thought you might be busy, and yes, Dax has been on a growth spurt; he and I have been praying for him to get taller."

"Tell me how that works because my grandson sure would like to be a little taller too."

"Well every night we pray:

And Jesus grew in wisdom and stature, and in favor with God and man. Luke 2:52.

We pray every night for him to grow just like Jesus, in wisdom, stature, and favor with God and man. All I know is it works. He is already nearly as tall as his dad."

Margaret motioned to Jane to come to the end of the counter nearest the kitchen. "Jane, I had a call from Lynn and Len. They get their tree for the Bed and Breakfast from me every year. They asked if I would go ahead and pick one out for them and see if you guys would mind bringing it back with yours. It will be just as easy to put two on top of your van."

"I know we used to get two or three trees from you and carry them all back on top of the van to Goose Creek with no trouble. How much do we owe you for the tree?" Jane answered as she pulled out her check book.

"Oh, you don't owe anything, Lynn said, she is paying for both trees since you are delivering hers."

"That's not fair we are going back there any way and we had planned to pay for our own tree."

"Nope, I can't let you do that, Lynn would never forgive me if I took your money. You also need to go over to the wreath shed and pick out two good size wreaths, one for Lynn and one to take home. They are on the house! Lynn sends me a bunch of business every year and you have bought a bunch of wreaths from me over the years. I think it's time you get a free one. Don't start any argument with me about this because you can't win!!"

Again, God had provided not just our needs but many of our wants.

Dale Warren

And my God will meet all your needs according to the riches of his glory in Christ Jesus.
Philippians 4:19

He had provided a home large enough for our expanded family, a handyman to fix it up, and now a tree and wreath to decorate the old house for Christmas. We should have known even more unexpected gifts and blessings were to come.

Dax announced, "The trees are on top of the van. Are you guys ready to go yet? I am starving!"

Jane finished picking out two wreaths, nearly taking as long as finding the perfect tree.

"Come on Jane, the kids are starving. They all look great just pick out two and let's go." I pleaded.

"I am not taking a wreath back to Lynn that is not round and has dead spots in it. She wouldn't do that to us. She deserves a great looking wreath. Don't you think?"

"Sure, but all those look great."

As she pulled two out from a stack in the back. "Okay, these two will do. Go ahead put them in the back of the van and tell the kids to use the restroom before we leave. We aren't stopping until we get back to the bed and breakfast."

THE RESCUE

No one will be able to stand against you all the days of your life. As I was with Moses, so I will be with you; I will never leave you nor forsake you.
Joshua 1:5

We arrived back at the bed and breakfast just as the sun was setting. Dax and I helped Len unload their tree off the roof of the van and carry it into the large den as Len kept thanking us for bringing back their tree. It was such a small thing to do to repay the hospitality and generosity of these two older missionaries.

Lynn yelled from the kitchen where she was watching a large pot of soup on the stove, singing a great old hymn, keeping time with the old wooden handled ladle on a heavy oak island in the middle of the kitchen. "You guys hungry? It's nothing fancy just some beef vegetable soup and some corn muffins." She cracked the stove door peeking in on the muffins like she was checking on a soft sleeping child and gently shutting the door back. "The soup is ready, and the muffins will need only a few more minutes. If you girls will come in and get out the bowls and fix some drinks, we can eat."

Serena and Dana quickly stepped into the kitchen and began pulling the bowls and plates out of an antique oak china cabinet. Dana asking, "Who wants tea for dinner?" Quickly she had taken all the drink orders as Serena placed the blue soup bowls on white china plates around the large dinner table. Dana finished filling the drink orders. "Jennifer, come place napkins at each place."

Dax and I finished placing the tree in a heavy cast iron tree stand. While I secured the tree by tightening the screws into the trunk of the tree.

Len handed Dax a brown plastic pitcher of water requesting, "Dax, while you are down there under the tree take this water and pour it in the stand."

Dax emptied the pitcher into the stand without spilling a single drop. We both crawled out from under the big tree that stood over ten feet high in the rustic den with pine paneling and a pitched ceiling with beams. Standing on each side of Len all three of us backed up with our hands on our hips admiring our accomplishment.

Unexpected Christmas

"Good job guys, I am getting too old to crawl down there on the floor. Let's wash up and get a bowl of that soup. I have been smelling it all afternoon."

Dax and I stood around the small pedestal sink washing our hands trying to remove the sticky pine tree sap without much success. Dax looked up and whispered. "Are we going to have to listen to the same old boring missionary stories again tonight?"

"You just sit there listen and show proper respect. Now let's go eat."

When Dax and I walked into the dining room, Jane, the girls, and Len were already sitting around the large table. Lynn was serving the soup into the bowls while Jane passed a platter of corn muffins around the table. Lynn finished filling the last bowl, sat down next to Len, and reached her hand over to Len's. Dana was sitting on the other side of Len. She took his hand completed the chain of hands around the table.

Len looked at me and asked, "Dale do you mind blessing this meal."

After a short blessing Lynn quickly interjected, "I hope you don't mind, it's not too fancy, just some vegetable soup and corn bread."

After we finished our second bowls of soup and before some could begin thirds, Jane stated, "Don't get too full. Lynn has apple pies in the kitchen. The apples were picked from her own trees in the back yard."

"Len, the first time I ever heard about you guys was years ago at church. We had special prayer for a couple of missionaries that were kidnapped. I never would have guessed we would meet you years later on a trip to the mountains for a Christmas tree and have a chance to share meals with heroes. But I have never heard the story from you. Are you comfortable sharing the incident with us?" I asked as dessert was being placed in front of us.

"Mr. Len, You were kidnapped!" Dax asked jumping up straight in his chair.

Len began explaining, "It is really a story not about us but about God and how he saved us. Lynn sit down and help me recount our experience. Lynn and I have served the Lord all over the world. First here in the states, then as missionaries in Thailand and then China, then finally in Africa. In Africa we were having house church meetings because we couldn't meet publicly without risking

Unexpected Christmas

the lives of Christians. The gangs and terrorist would threaten anyone who worshipped Christ with death or torture. We would move the meetings around to protect those that were coming to pray and worship the Lord. In one of the meeting just as we were finishing our prayer time, we heard a rumble right in front of the house. It was two vehicles, a large black car and an older black pick-up truck that drove right into the front yard of the house. Several men in green camouflage uniforms jumped out of the car and out of the back of the pick-up. A couple of the men stood outside the house between the front door and the truck, while three of the men busted the door open. Some of the worshipers ran out the back but most of the faithful people with us stood their ground with a couple of the women dropping to their knees to pray. One of the guerrillas pointed his rifle right at Lynn and I and barked, 'You two come with us.' One of the older men in the group shouted at the gunman. 'You can't take them. They haven't done anything wrong. All we were doing was praying for our people including you.' The guerrilla shouted back. 'You know that is forbidden.' One of the men had circled around behind us and began pushing me and Lynn out the front door. The next thing we knew they tied our hands, put hoods over our heads, and forced us into the trunk of the big black car."

Dax had been focused on every word even sliding up to the edge of his chair. "They did all that just because you were praying. Miss Lynn were you scared? What did you do?"

Lynn picked up the story. "Believe it or not we were pretty calm. God just seemed to give us a peace. I figured the worst that could happen I would be killed. I was tied up right next to Len and if we were killed, we would be together in heaven with Jesus. But one of the women that was at the prayer meeting remembered a Pastor friend of ours who had come over the year before to work with us. She remembered what city he was from and the name of his church. She called around until she got a hold of him and explained what had happened and asked him to have his church pray. Well, he did much more. He contacted the mission board and in no time churches all over the country were praying and not just churches, but seminaries and Christian colleges, schools, and workplaces were stopping and praying for our rescue."

Unexpected Christmas

Jane looked at the children that were all staring in amazement at this couple that they knew best as innkeepers and great cooks in an entirely different light. Now they weren't just a nice older couple that cooked the best gingerbread pancakes and apple pie they had ever tasted but now they were suddenly action heroes. Sure, missionaries passed out Bibles, held prayer meetings, and taught people English. But Lynn and Len had battled death squads and evil.

Jane responded, "I remember the morning I got that prayer request from our prayer coordinator at First Baptist Goose Creek. I had never met them but suddenly they became close family members that needed our prayers. I sat down the phone and prayed for them. Then I called your Dad at his office and asked him to start praying."

"Mom let them finish the story. How did you get out of that trunk?" Dax asked raising himself up and sitting on his legs to get closer to the missionary hero.

Len took a sip of tea and continued the story. "Lynn and I just laid in that dark cold trunk praying. Dax, do you remember the story of Daniel in the fiery furnace?"

"Yes, when they looked in the furnace Jesus was in there with him."

"Well, Lynn and I knew we were not in that trunk alone. A few times over the next day they would stop the car pull us out and threaten to kill us. Then they would throw us back in the trunk. Then after 24 hours the car slammed on brakes. Two of the men pulled us out of the trunk and cut the ropes off our wrist. They appeared to be frightened as they jumped back into the car and sped away. We had no idea what had happened or why instead of killing us they had suddenly freed us and drove away frightened."

Lynn spoke up as she slid her chair around next to Len and placed her hand on his arm. "Let me tell them what happened when the kidnappers were captured about three weeks later. Three of the men all shared the same story about that night. They suddenly had a change of plans and released us. One of the men explained, their car was surrounded by giants over ten feet tall with flaming swords that forced the car to the side of the road. The other two men confirmed the encounter about giants with flaming swords."

Unexpected Christmas

Serena who usually tuned these boring missionary stories out but had been focused on every word this time, shouted out. "What was it?"

"God had answered all those prayers from around the world by sending an army of HIS angels. I am sure they were being led by the same Commander of the Lord's Army that appeared to Joshua before the battle of Jericho. There is no doubt in our minds that we were rescued by an army of angels. Now you guys have a long ride back tomorrow, you better start getting in bed." Lynn shared.

Dana asked, "What about the tree? Aren't we supposed to help decorate it tonight?"

"It's late. We can decorate in the morning while Len fixes breakfast. We will get all the decorations out and have them ready to start first thing in the morning." Lynn stated as we began getting up from the table.

The next morning the kids woke up in their normal order and attitudes. First Dana and Caroline rolled out hesitantly and obediently. We must get up, so we might as well rollout. Serena and Jennifer surrendered after the third time they were reminded to get up and begin getting ready. Dax shot out of his bed ready to take on the world.

Jane assumed her drill sergeant mode, "You guys get moving. Get dressed, pack your bags, put them at the door, get down here, and let's get started on Lynn's tree. Nobody is eating breakfast until we get packed up and finish decorating the tree."

Quickly the three oldest girls placed their assorted bags at the front door. They moved over and began helping check each strand of lights as we draped the lights around the tree. Jane adding her usual instructions. "Take each string all the way in to the trunk and back out on every limb."

Serena sitting on the floor cross legged surrounded by a string of lights announced the obvious, "Where is Dax and Jennifer, aren't they supposed to be helping."

"Dax is in the kitchen helping Len with breakfast." Jane explained.

Dana's response, "You mean he is already eating breakfast, while we are working."

Dax defending himself from the kitchen. "I have not ate! I am helping so we can all eat!" While he finished off a piece of bacon.

Unexpected Christmas

Then from upstairs Jennifer with her best tired whiney voice, "I can't come down my bag is too heavy, if I try to bring it downstairs, I will fall and break my neck."

I responded, "Okay, just leave it up there, I will come get it."

Dana shaking her head, "Dad, don't give in to her whining. She can bring that downstairs. Mom, I bet if you go up there, she is laying on her bed still in her pajamas."

"Jennifer get down here right now your sisters are doing all the work." Jane ordered.

"Okay, I will be down just give me a minute. I need to use the bathroom, first."

Serena had heard enough, "See she hasn't done anything to get ready. I'm not doing anymore until her and Dax do their share."

Dax said, "Breakfast is done. You guys come into the kitchen and place your order for your omelets. We got swiss cheese, cheddar cheese, tomatoes, mushrooms, onions, bacon, or ham. Toast, coffee, or juice is on the table."

Serena answered, "I don't want all that stuff just give me the ham and cheese. Yellow cheese."

The other kids began moving into the kitchen each taking a turn ordering their custom omelets.

Len responded, "Dale, go ahead and bless the breakfast so everyone can begin eating before the breakfast gets cold."

After a quick blessing, thanking the Lord and our gracious host each of us began coming out of the kitchen holding a plate with their own custom designed omelet sitting it down on the table and claiming a glass of orange juice or cold white milk.

After finishing the last omelet and making sure nobody needed a second one, Len came in and sat his plate at the head of the table which had been saved for the chief omelet cooker and missionary hero.

Dax as usual took a huge slice of butter and began to spread it on his toast like he was spreading frosting on a wedding cake. "Dax that's enough! Scrape some of that butter off and hand me the knife for my toast." Jane commanded.

"Dax, you did a great job helping with breakfast. You kept saying you wanted to ask me something, but I had my hands full fixing breakfast. What is it?" Len asked as he finally was able to begin eating his breakfast.

"Well, I still don't get it. You were seriously rescued by giant angels with flaming swords?" Dax asked in his most serious voice.

"Dax, you have been misled like most people about angels. It all begins with the cute children's nativities we see every year. Have you ever participated in one of those programs at church?"

"Sure, nearly every year. I usually play a shepherd, but I have been a wiseman and one year I even played a sheep."

"You never played an angel?"

Jennifer finally had made it to the table and spoke for the first time. "Yeh, Dax was never an angel. If he had played an angel, everyone would have laughed their heads off."

Dax responded, "Girls always played the angels."

"Yes, we have propagated this misconception about God's messengers by always having some cute little girl in a white robe with white or silver wings bordered with fringe. But if you read what the Bible says about the angels at Christmas it is an entirely different picture."

While Len talked Lynn reached over to the bookcase in the corner of the dining room and pulled out a large black Bible. She carefully opened the large book with yellowing pages and thumbed through the pages carefully handling the pages until she stopped and tracked her finger about a third of the way down the page.

Lynn said, "Let me read you this passage from the "real" Christmas story in Luke chapter two."

She began, "**And there were shepherds living out in the fields nearby, keeping watch over their flocks at night. ⁹ An angel of the Lord appeared to them, and the glory of the Lord shone around them, and they were terrified. Luke 2:8-9"**

She looked up and continued. "First, shepherds were bad dudes, Dax. They worked out in fields during all kinds of weather often alone handling any emergency and protecting their sheep from wolves, lions, thieves, etc. If a little girl or a little smiling cherub had showed up do you think those tough men would have been **terrified?** I don't think so, but if a ten-foot tall warrior with a flaming sword showed up I can see them being scared. Have you ever noticed how all the accounts about angels showing up begin with the angels saying, **'Fear Not!'** When we need protection or rescuing, God can send an army of those warriors."

Unexpected Christmas

No one will be able to stand against you all the days of your life. As I was with Moses, so I will be with you; I will never leave you nor forsake you.
Joshua 1:5

We finished breakfast, helped string the lights on their tree, and hung a few old ornaments while getting dressed for church with the Whiteheads. Later that morning our children watched the two missionaries lead a small congregation of believers in worship that with an entirely different perspective. They weren't just two older folks singing old hymns in an old church with mostly older people sitting quietly in their pews. No, the service was now being led by two heroes of the faith. Two brave missionaries that trusted in Jesus even when faced with armed terrorist and locked in a dark damp car trunk. Because even in those circumstances they knew the greatest gift and blessing is God's presence in all our circumstances. When the last hymn was sung and a few hugs. We pulled out of the gravel drive way in the Silver Bullet with our tree strapped to the top of the car. Unexpectantly we had come for a tree but left with something much more important and valuable the true meaning of Christmas. Christ had come to dwell among HIS people and HIS Presence is still here with HIS people.

THE CARD – THE GIFT – THE BLESSING

Now to him who is able to do immeasurably more than all we ask or imagine, according to his power that is at work within us, Ephesians 3:20

We arrived back home with our tree, wrestled it off the top of the van, and placed it in its stand in a corner next to the fireplace in the living room of the old white house. This year like most we had slightly under estimated the height of the ceiling, so after trimming a small piece off the top of the tree our angel would just fit on the top with her head barely brushing the ceiling. This slight brush with the ceiling caused the angel to lean forward just enough that she appeared to be looking down on us. A reminder that God's angels were constantly watching over us. This angel might be a beautiful woman with a flowing burgundy dress trimmed in white fur. She could have represented a snow queen from Dr. Zhivago, but this angel like all God's angels most importantly represented the presence of God in our lives.

The next night we followed our annual tradition of each fixing mugs of hot chocolate. Some mugs seemed to have more marshmallows than hot chocolate. We listened to Bing Crosby and Nat King Cole Christmas music while sipping our hot chocolate and decorating the tree following Jane's careful instructions for trimming the perfect tree. Once the tree was completed, we all sat back on the couch, chairs, and floor to admire our work. A tree adorned with an assortment of children's ornaments, wooden German ornaments, expensive Hallmark ornaments and of course the hand-painted ornaments*. As I looked at the bottom of my empty mug the tree was nearly perfect. The lights arranged evenly around the tree with the ornaments placed carefully to showcase the most important ones up front.

I decided to ask a question. "Do you kids know why we use a Christmas tree to celebrate Christmas?"

Dana as usual the first to answer, "I know Martin Luther had the first Christmas tree in Germany."

Unexpected Christmas

"Yes, that is what tradition tells us. He went out in the snow-covered forest cut it down and brought it home."

The other kids then began excitingly adding to the conversation. "It's an evergreen to represent eternal life. The lights represent the "light of the world".

After a few more answers I announced, "It's late. Time for everyone to go to bed, tomorrow we are back to school and work."

When things quieted down, and everyone had made their last trip to the bathroom or to the kitchen for one more drink of water. I sat looking at the beautiful tree realizing there was only one thing missing to complete this representation of Christ's love for us. There were no presents under the tree or money to purchase presents. The presents we exchange at Christmas represent the greatest gift that was ever given, our Lord Jesus Christ.

For to us a child is born, to us a son is given, and the government will be on his shoulders. And he will be called Wonderful Counselor,

Dale Warren

Mighty God, Everlasting Father, Prince of Peace. Isaiah 9:6

Could any gift ever compare to the WONDERFUL COUNSELOR, MIGHTY GOD, EVERLASTING FATHER and PRINCE OF PEACE – God gave us that first Christmas – The Presence of God in our lives.

After our return from the mountains and a great Thanksgiving weekend decorating for the holidays, it was time to get back to class and work schedules. Our family had borrowed a tradition we had learned from a friend at church. When we received Christmas cards, we would open the cards at dinner read them together as a family, pray for the person or family that had sent them, and place them in a basket in the center of the dining room table. After opening the new card, we would pull one or more of the cards from the basket and pray for that family.

I finished a New Testament exam and a drudge through another boring lecture on Church History. My next stop would be to go by check the mail and race to the car, so I could quickly get to one of my three part-time jobs. I nodded and waved at a few friends and classmates as I walked quickly through

Unexpected Christmas

the student building not daring to stop for a conversation knowing there is no such thing as a quick conversation when two pastors or future pastors say just got a minute. I avoided the delays and arrived at my mailbox. Glancing inside through the small window in the front of the box I noticed several pieces of mail. Opening the box, I pulled out an electric bill. I was thinking maybe wait for later to open it knowing it has been cooler since the last one and the electric heaters really run up the bill. Next was a reminder of Christmas activities on campus, like I ever have time for the social activities on campus. Then a couple of brightly colored envelopes that must be Christmas cards. I had better not open those without the whole family around the dinner table.

Then finally that night after everyone was home, we settled around the dinner table. Jane had prepared a meatloaf with mashed potatoes but before we ate, I pulled out the three cards. Looking at the return addresses one was from a former neighbor, another was from one of our cousins, and the last one from a Mrs. Carson. We looked at each other with a little confusion.

Dax asked, "Who is that? Where did it come from?"

I answered the best I could, "I'm not sure. Her address is Goose Creek. Jane do you know, Mrs. Carson?"

"No, I can't remember a Mrs. Carson from Goose Creek."

Jennifer interrupted, "Let's open them and have our prayer."

Dana added, "Yeh, so we can eat; some of us still have homework to finish."

We opened the first two cards and passed them around the table. Jane commenting on each one with the same response. "Aren't they beautiful."

Then I opened the third card. It was another beautiful card solid blue with a huge star in the corner and three kings on camels marching towards a small stable in the bottom corner of the card. Across the top of the card in silver block letters "Wisemen still seek HIM!" Then as I opened the card there was something in the card. I thought at first another of those Christmas family newsletters about everything the family had done over the last year. No, this wasn't one of those boring letters. It was a blank sheet of paper with a

Unexpected Christmas

check folded in half tucked inside the paper. I unfolded the check and was speechless.

Jane reached her hand towards the check and asked, "Well, how much is it? Oh, my goodness!"

Jane laid the check in the center of the table with tears running down her cheeks.

Jennifer responded, "Mom, are you okay?"

"I am fine. God is so good!"

Caroline and Dana leaned over the table and at the same time asked, "Is that a thousand dollars?"

Serena echoed, "A thousand dollars."

I turned to Jane, "You will have to call your mom and ask her who is Mrs. Carson. How does she know us?"

"I'll call as soon as we finish eating. Nana knows everyone in Goose Creek. She will be able to solve the mystery of Mrs. Carson."

We all loved Jane's meatloaf but tonight it tasted better than ever. Jane called her mom and found out Mrs. Carson was one of the ladies in Nana's Sunday School Class. Jane got her phone number from Nana, we wanted to call her and thank her for the generous gift.

I took the phone and dialed the number. After a few rings it was answered. I heard an older woman's voice on the phone. I identified myself, "Mrs. Carson this is Dale Walker, Modine's son-in-law."

She responded, "Hi, how are you guys."

"We are wonderful. We received your card today and just wanted to call and thank you for this gift. You didn't have to do that for us."

"We pray for your family every Sunday in our Sunday School Class and Modine keeps us up to date on your progress each week. The Lord just kept telling me to send you the check. I know there are always extra expenses at Christmas, but if you don't need it," she answered.

I interjected quickly, "Oh, we can certainly use it. You have been an answer to our prayers for help. I am so glad you responded to God as he spoke to you."

"Well I better let you go before we run up your phone bill. I don't want you to have to use it to pay a high phone bill. I will continue to pray for you."

I finished, "Goodbye and God bless you."

God had answered another prayer and as usual HIS actions are even greater than we expect. There would now be presents under the tree to celebrate

Unexpected Christmas

the birth of HIM who answered all our prayers beyond our expectations.

Now to him who is able to do immeasurably more than all we ask or imagine, according to his power that is at work within us, Ephesians 3:20

Our family had left the comfort of our home and security of a corporate position and paycheck to follow Christ to seminary expecting many hardships. God showed us again and again that when following HIM in faith we continued to experience many unexpected gifts and blessings and most importantly HIS presence constantly in our lives.

The thief cometh not, but for to steal, and to kill, and to destroy: I am come that they might have life, and that they might have it more abundantly. John 10:10

*Hand Painted Ornaments by Dale Warren published 2017

Dale Warren

AN APPLE IN YOUR STOCKING

After Job had prayed for his friends, the LORD restored his fortunes and gave him twice as much as he had before. Job 42:10

After all the many unexpected gifts and blessings, God still had another blessing still to come. On Christmas, after opening presents and a huge meal, we began to unwind and think about all the blessings we had received since making the decision to follow Christ. We had been receiving phone calls all day from family and church family wishing us a Merry Christmas and to just let us know we were loved and missed.

Then late that afternoon, the phone rang, and Jane answered. "Yes, this is Jane. Sami, I can't believe it's you. We haven't seen you and John in ages. Where are you and what are you doing."

We had met John and Sami while we were all stationed in Germany. Two young couples, one from South Carolina and the other from Ohio that grew to become best friends for life. Jane taught Sami how to prepare cornbread dressing and pecan pie. Sami instructed Jane on how to fix ribs and bread stuffing. John was a helicopter mechanic/pilot that could repair anything and to prove it he restored an old VW van. We traveled all over Europe in the van that only a miracle mechanic could keep on the road.

Sami began to explain, "We are stationed at Ft. Eustis in Virginia. I tried calling your number in Goose Creek and it was disconnected. Luckily, I had kept your mother's number from when we were in Germany. I called it this morning and your mom told me about you guys going to seminary at Wake Forest. Well, John and I are living in Virginia not too far from you. I was wondering if you had plans for tomorrow. I know for us the day after Christmas is usually free."

Jane still so excited couldn't answer fast enough. "Sure, we are going to be home all day. No school or work tomorrow. Let me know what time you will be here. What do you guys want for dinner?"

"Nothing let me bring the stuff to fix my special BBQ ribs. Are they still Dale's favorite?" Sami responded.

"You know Dale, he loves Sami's ribs. I still use the recipe you taught me in Germany and everyone raves about how tender my ribs are. I am a little embarrassed to tell them a Yankee taught this southern girl how to make the best pork ribs."

"No, let me bring everything for the dinner. You fix desserts. Now John wants to talk to Dale for a minute."

Jane handed me the phone. "John how are you guys doing. I overheard Jane and Sami. I can't wait to see you guys. How many years has it been?"

John responded, "Better not try to guess Sami and Jane will think they are getting old. Tell me all about seminary. I am not surprised I knew God had a plan for you guys, but Dale your background was accounting. Are you now going to be a preacher? I have already checked it out and from Ft. Eustis to Wake Forest is only about three hours, so we should be able to get out of here in the morning and be there about noon."

I spent the next few minutes telling John all about the night Christ called me into the ministry.

Then I told him how everything had worked out for our transition. I told him God certainly has a since of humor calling this guy that only wanted to work with numbers to now be a preacher. I am now writing papers and giving sermons something, I never would have guessed possible. I finished said our goodbyes and started planning with Jane for the next day.

When noon arrived the next day, Sami called explaining they were running a bit late, but John had one stop he had to make in Raleigh. She promised to be in soon and John had a surprise for Dale.

Jane answered the door with huge hugs for Sami and John. "Sami, you look great. Where are the kids? I wanted to see how much they had grown."

"We left them with their grandparents. John and I wanted a quiet peaceful drive today. Plus, the grandparents wanted a chance to spoil them a little before they have to go back to school."

John always seemed to stand back a bit and let Sami have the spotlight. Like many great men and heroes, I have known John seemed to be humble not needing the spotlight, but anyone who worked with him or knew him for a while realized he was a very special man.

John holding up a large red Christmas stocking. "Dale, you told us many times your grandfather always gave you and your brothers fruit at Christmas, so I brought you a special gift." John handed me the stocking. "Merry Christmas."

Thanking John, we all walked into the house as I looked in the stocking filled with oranges, grapefruit, and apples.

Jane responded, "Grapefruit, you remembered, it is my favorite."

John added, "I know it's not your favorite, Dale but I thought you and the kids would enjoy the oranges and apples. I have some more in the car. Let me go out and get it."

Sami excitedly, "Yes, John go get it. Get it now!"

I turned to John, "Can I help you?"

"No, I got it just sit right here and I will be right back in." He looked over at Dax and said, "Dax hold the door for me when I come back."

John pulled a large box out of the back of their car and began carrying it up on the porch.

Dax swung open the door. "What is that? Is it what I think? Who is it for?"

Unexpected Christmas

John had just walked in the door with a large white box with "APPLE II" printed on the side with the famous apple logo just below. I was not quite as naïve as Dax. I knew John had probably gotten a new computer for Christmas and was just using the box to bring in Sami's dinner fixings.

John responded to Dax's question, "It is for your Dad, but I guess your whole family can use it. When your dad told me, he was still typing his papers on an electric typewriter, I couldn't sleep last night. I woke up early this morning and started looking in the paper and calling around for an after Christmas sale on computers. When Sami woke up, I told her what I had found, and she agreed we needed to do something. We stopped in Raleigh this morning and picked this up. I thought Dale could use one more "APPLE" in his stocking."

"John that is too much. Those things are too expensive." I said as tears came to my eyes.

Sami responded, "Years ago you and Jane did a great expensive favor for us and when we tried to not accept it. Do you know what Jane said? She said, 'Don't steal our blessing by not accepting it.' Don't steal John and my blessing. We are just excited we could do something to help you follow God's call."

John asked, "Dax, can you help me set, this thing up? Where can we set it up?"

"Dad has a desk in his room. Let's set it up in there."

Jane interrupted, "Dale, you better get in there first and clear off a place. That desk top always looks like a tornado went over it."

"Here John let me go first and clear off the desk. Then you will have to show us how to use it."

Sami watched all the girls standing around in awe. "Once they get it set up all of you can check it out. I am sure it will help all of you with your school work."

Unexpected Christmas

Dax interrupted, "It has games too, like pong."

Sami stood up and asked, "Who wants to help me get the dinner out of the car and start fixing the ribs?"

After a great dinner where we all ate too many ribs. We each took a turn with the new computer and catching up on all the things that had transpired since seeing each other. The best thing about these old friends are years can pass between times we see each other and in a few minutes it's like we were just together last week.

We tried our best to convince John and Sami to stay over. Dax even explained the house is warmer since Carlos installed insulation and closed-up the big holes in the floor. But even with our best attempts, they explained that they promised to be back that night to pick-up the children.

After their car backed out of the drive way, we sat down in the "Old White House" and began to reflect on all our gifts and blessings from our first Christmas following God.

I asked the children, "Why do you think God continues to bring such special people into our lives and use them to bless us."

Dale Warren

They all answered together. "I guess God just loves us!" This was certainly an unexpected Christmas of gifts and blessings.

GRACE
God's Riches At Christ's Expense

Merry Christmas
The Warrens

MY TESTIMONY

God has a plan for your life.

"For I know the plans I have for you," declares the LORD, "plans to prosper you and not to harm you, plans to give you hope and a future."
Jeremiah 29:11

I wasn't raised in a family that attended church regularly. My parents believed in God, Jesus, and the Bible. I was raised to believe and trust in what I call the American Dream theology. If you stayed out of trouble, got a good education, and worked hard; you would be happy, and your life would be complete. After I dropped out of college and was drafted, I married my teenage sweet-heart. We spent seven years in the army, then moved back to our home town and returned to her home church, First Baptist Goose Creek. It was what was expected. I had completed my MBA while in the army, so I got out the army, took a corporate job, started going to church, and trying my best to be a good father and husband. I was still searching for that full and meaningful life.

Dale Warren

Then one night my sister and brother-in-law (Dale and Kim Hawkins) invited Jane and I over for dinner. After dinner I sat down to begin watching a Braves baseball game with Brother Dale.

Just as the game began, he asked, "What seems to be the problem? You just seem frustrated."

I answered, "I don't know, it just seems the more I try, it is never be enough. I can't explain it, but I just seem to be frustrated with life."

Brother Dale continued, "Well let me ask you a question. If you died tonight, would you go to heaven?"

I thought a moment that is a pretty personal question, before answering. "I guess I would."

Brother Dale responded, "Guessing is not good enough." Pointing to the TV, he continued, "I guess the Braves will win tonight but if they don't it won't matter because they play again tomorrow night. But where you spend eternity is the most important decision you will ever make."

"I think I will go to heaven. I am a good person and try to be a good father and husband." I explained.

Brother Dale answered, "Eternity is not something to guess, wish, or think about it is something you should KNOW! The Bible states: ***"I write these things to you who believe in the name of the Son of God so that you may <u>know</u> that you have eternal life." 1 John 5:13.***

The key was I could know that God loved me and would never leave me. He would be the guide for my life, now and for eternity.

I then prayed with Dale for God to forgive me of my sins and accept me into HIS family. On that day I began a new relationship with Jesus. Jesus became not just my Lord and Savior, but my best friend and constant companion. I began a new life where everything did not depend on me, but I could trust Jesus. That night I instantly found a peace I had never felt before.

I can now trust Jesus to guide my life and know that God has planned a life for me – a full and meaningful life. - ***The thief comes only to steal and kill and destroy; I have come that they may have life and have it more abundantly. John 10:10***

That is why I always tell people Dale Hawkins introduced me to the two most important people in my life, Jesus and Jane. If you would like to discuss how Jesus can provide a peace in your life or would like to share how HIS presence in your life has filled you with a peace, please feel free to contact:

Rev Dale Warren, daleabbawarren@yahoo.com.

For I know the plans I have for you," declares the LORD, "plans to prosper you and not to harm you, plans to give you hope and a future.
Jeremiah 29:11

Made in the USA
Columbia, SC
26 November 2018